Murder and Homicide IX

Peter J. Michael

Murder and Homicide IX

ISBN-13: 978-1-923666-26-9

Published by Peter J. Michael

ALL BOOKS BY THIS AUTHOR ARE:

THE GREAT WAR AGAINST TERRORISM

KILLING THE BOGEYMAN I & II

RUTHLESS

RELIGIOUS DEATH TRAP

THE GOD OF ELIMINATION

THE MURDEROUS MR. A

MADMAN'S RETURN

MURDER AND HOMICIDE I - IX

Part 'nine' of the Murder and Homicide cops versus villains' fiction book series.

Murder and Homicide IX

MURDER AND HOMICIDE IX

CHAPTER 1

Robert Stewart was on an escalated pursuit to identify great threats and significant risks to innocent bystanders and properties throughout the entire city and state of New York. Robert Stewart carefully strategized his master plans to combat his awful foe's determined chaos and mayhem agendas, to target many individuals and their organisations he deemed as responsible for the death of his son, he titled, George the Great.

And thus, Robert Stewart not only had to identify all targets being threatened by Domenico Armando, but at the same time, he had to protect the safeties of a great many innocent people and their properties that may end up being decimated and destroyed in the process of Domenico Armando's 'Great War' he planned in the city and state of New York.

Robert Stewart was driving his unmarked civilian vehicle across the entire State of New

York, as if he was intentionally looking for trouble, with piercing eyes gazing left and right, as he drove across the city's streets looking for potential killer armies and henchmen of Domenico Armando, ready to strike hundreds and thousands of targets at a whim, via the severely brutal orders of their tragically demonic and powerfully explosive Padrone Master Domenico Armando!

Robert Stewart was ready in advance for Domenico Armando's bloody wrath and retributive actions to be unleashed in New York effective immediately.

Domenico Armando wanted revenge against the whole host of people he blamed as responsible for the recent death of his son George. And those targets were every medical practitioner doctor and practising nurse that occupied the inside boundaries of the city and state, full stop.

Robert Stewart understood Domenico Armando's plans ahead of schedule. Robert Stewart sensed instinctively that Domenico Armando wanted to target and eliminate brutally so, every doctor and every nurse within New York's borders he not only categorised as reckless and incompetent, but downright negligent and horrendously corrupt in administering their medical duties to not only his deceased son, but on many of their patients, contributing to all their deaths. Especially the considered murder of his son George!

Domenico Armando classified that all doctors were frauds, sick maniacs, lunatics and the worst killers that society endorsed as legalised criminals responsible for more people's deaths in their totality, than any and all dictators in the history of humanity had ever managed to accomplish combined! Furthermore, Robert Stewart remarkably was not oblivious to sharing the same judgement when it became known that medical practitioners were also targeting him, Commander Robert Stewart himself, for elimination.

Robert Stewart already had surveillance cast on identified criminal doctors in the city through his investigation, in which he uncovered ingeniously, such criminal medical practitioners were also targeting his life, wanting to kill him as they had been responsible for killing masses of their patients and getting away with it for years on end.

The irony of Robert Stewart's investigation into the sordid ordeal, was that not only was he burdened with identifying Domenico Armando's mass murderous plots against every medical practitioner in the entire city of New York, but also at the same time, Robert Stewart was on a fervent quest to neutralise through his exhaustive investigations, every corrupt medical authority roaming throughout the city and state, who not only were deliberately causing the deaths of their patients through negligence and corruption, but also at the same time, certain members of the medical community he was hunting, who began targeting him for elimination for his past actions as a cop, which resulted in his incarceration of their specific relatives, who were on top of it, criminals themselves!

It seemed as though Robert Stewart's investigations into Domenico Armando's mass murderous plots against doctors at present, had as well systematically unearthed a Pandora's Box of troublesome activities being instigated and perpetrated by the Domenico Armando targeted medical practitioners themselves, who were also guilty of plotting and scheming to commit murder against a police officer, which was outside the usual scope of their medical duties. These horrendous medical misfits were proving very rapidly to be responsible for masses of their patients being killed. So not only were the doctors responsible for killing their patients, but certain doctors were also responsible for plotting and planning the death and demise of a specific famous cop in the city called Robert Stewart.

Robert Stewart's investigation was quickly growing in scope. His surveillance operations were unearthing one scam of troublesome activities after another; all pointed to the medical practitioners in New York. The doctors were enjoying the money they were receiving from their patients, for giving them an incompetent medical service, at the same time as the doctors intended to cover up their crimes, by killing or planning to kill a cop who was responsible for the incarceration of some of their relatives, in fear that this specific cop in question named Robert Stewart, would also target such criminal doctors and uncover all their misdeeds of mass slaughter and medical neglect, as well as improper medications being prescribed to their unknowing patients, who would die from the side effects of such medical corruption being thusly administered to them, one by one and in masses every single day throughout such horrendously corrupt doctors' medical practises.

How did Robert Stewart uncover these medical practitioners planned plots of assassination against him? It all began with incarcerated corrupt police officer Elliot Archer. Elliot Archer who was arrested by

Robert Stewart recently for accepting bribes by the Armando family was kept under surveillance inside his prison lockup facility awaiting trial for his police corruption activities he was being charged for.

Robert Stewart intercepted a specific visitor making an inhumane appearance outside Elliot Archer's prison holding cell, located at the 25th division precinct station house in Brooklyn, New York. And the conversations which ensued between Elliot Archer and this specific visitor were most certainly enlightening, if not repulsively earth-shattering. This specific visitor was a psychiatrist whose name was Steven Archer, incarcerated corrupt cop Elliot Archer's older brother of three years. Elliot Archer's brother was 43 years old and much like his younger brother Elliot, he was also slender built but with wavy thick brown hair. And Steven Archer was a certified practising psychiatrist in the borough of Queens, New York. He came to the jail cell of his brother Elliot Archer to offer his assistance. And the assistance he offered was to help eliminate all threats against his brother, via his planned conspiracies to commit murder against the cop Robert Stewart who was responsible for his arrest and current incarceration behind bars.

Ex-officer Elliot Archer must have been a very stupid person as well as a corrupt cop Robert Stewart considered. The conversations he had with his brother and vice versa were not censored at the very least. The conversations were deliberately open and bloody murderous in their connotations, as if they were allowed to speak freely unmonitored.

Robert Stewart thought that Elliot Archer, the incarcerated corrupt cop, was one dumb son of a bitch. This stupid bastard should have known that his conversations would be monitored during his arrest and incarceration in the local lockup facility pending trial, and the outcome to that trial, was most definite to conclude in a well-deserved conviction and an exorbitant prison sentencing for his horrible crimes, which would come to pass through the damning evidence compiled against him of such crimes, which led to his arrest.

But Elliot Archer did not caution his brother to censor his conversations. No. Elliot Archer instead, spoke freely inside the prison lockup facility, as if he had nothing to worry about. Elliot Archer condoned and even encouraged his psychiatrist brother Steven Archer to participate in the planned murder of

7

Commander Robert Stewart behind his, Elliot Archer's certain demise.

The conversations between the two were open, direct, incriminating and damning furthermore, to not only Elliot Archer's upcoming trial, where he would be indicted with further charges and additional crimes, now concerning the conspired murder of his arrestor, but also his brother Psychiatrist Steven Archer, was automatically implicated so easily through his incriminating words and conspired actions to assist his brother's departure from prison, he so hoped in his mind, delusionally would occur, by killing the one threat to his brother's freedom, Commander Robert Stewart. The whole sordid affair was a joke Robert thought to himself. Those two stupid idiots had just signed their own death warrants, Robert visualised the scenario in his mind so clearly through their horribly incriminating and stupidly planned conspiracies quite openly and publicly in an jail facility, they were either oblivious or ignorant that anything they said or did together at such a facility was being monitored and recorded, both audibly and visually at that!

Robert Stewart listened to the conversations taking place between the two horrendously stupid brothers proceed as if there was nothing to worry about, with spoken words exchanged between the pair both standing and staring at each other in the prison facility's cell division. Elliot Archer was inside his cell, and his brother Steven Archer was standing outside the jail cell talking freely and talking murder of a police commander responsible for Elliot Archer's would-be demise and certain destruction. Robert Stewart would listen and watch the surveillance recordings of the two brothers proceed unashamedly between the two Archer sibling morons, crucifying themselves and hanging themselves systematically and carelessly in the process of their outspoken words and deliberate attempts, to conspire to commit murder against a man they saw as a great threat against them titled, Commander Robert Stewart!

CHAPTER 2

Robert Stewart listened to the two Archer brothers' words and self-incriminating conspiracies literally resulting in the two of them crucifying themselves! And through these conversations, and conspired actions of murder, Robert Stewart most certainly opened up a Pandora's Box of widespread medical corruption in the city and state of New York, which not only included and was responsible for medical practitioners' neglect and corruption killing their patients by the masses, but also included the conspiracies and planned cold-blooded murders outside their practises of anyone they deemed a threat to them. And that threat right now was targeted against Commander Robert Stewart.

It was instantly uncovered, that certain doctors including Psychiatrist Steven Archer wanted to result in Robert Stewart being removed from the planet so to speak, and being sent screaming to a gruesome fate - and then witness it thereafter in his own death memorial service!

In such corrupt medical practitioners' minds such as Psychiatrist Steven Archer,

Commander Robert Stewart's death would solve a hell of a lot of problems for them all. And in Psychiatrist Steven Archer's very sick and twisted mindset, Robert Stewart's death would also automatically result in all charges being dropped against his incarcerated corrupt cop brother Elliot Archer, which would automatically conclude, as a matter of course, in Elliot Archer's apparent freedom taking place. Psychiatrist Steven Archer was truly naïve, unrealistic, gullible and self-sabotaging in his very poor judgments and dire assessment of the entire situation! Because no matter what, the evidence against his brother Elliot Archer was undeniable. He did not think that the murder of Commander Robert Stewart would alter nothing where his brother Elliot Archer's current fate was concerned. Elliot Archer would remain behind bars no matter what. And he would be convicted in a court of law receiving a hefty prison sentence regardless of his plans to commit murder, a horrible murder, a bloody murder, a gruesome murder against the cop behind Elliot Archer's incarceration, who went by the name of Commander Robert Stewart. This sorry excuse of a fool Psychiatrist Steven Archer was truly a horrible medical doctor for complex mental health conditions in general. He was a terrible psychiatrist! He proved to be extremely poor in his assessments and poor in his judgments in understanding the nature of psychiatry in general. A psychiatrist was meant to identify truths and patterns of human behaviours leading to such truths. But Psychiatrist Steven Archer knew nothing about the field he received the qualification to practise: psychiatry. Steven Archer was ignorant. He was a fake. He was a phoney, a fraud. And now the evidence mounted against him had proven that he was also a man capable of murder; at the very least, conspiring to commit murder; and against a well-regarded cop at that!

So, Robert's evidence against medical corruption throughout his own investigations was building rather rapidly. Robert Stewart did not arrest Psychiatrist Steven Archer immediately. He kept the sonofabitch under surveillance. He wanted a 24-hour tail on him to see where he went, who he spoke to. And Robert's instincts to keep him roaming free for now under tight watch proved very lucrative to his investigations. Robert Stewart identified through his investigations, a legion of medical corruption, when in not too long a period thereafter, Psychiatrist Steven Archer was clearly witnessed and heard, through telephone conversations, all his phone calls tapped, that he was enlisting the cooperation of other psychiatrists, and even talk therapy psychologists throughout the city and state of New York, to assist in pooling resources together and monies, so they could afford to pay the most expensive hitman to do the job of murder against Commander Robert Stewart.

Medical Doctor Psychiatrist Steven Archer understood that organising a hit against the cop in question was no cheap feat for anyone. It would cost a hell of a lot of money. And Psychiatrist Steven Archer was also a greedy sonofabitch as well as a corrupt fraud. He was the exact opposite, the antonym of the word bona fide. Psychiatrist Steven Archer was not authentic and certainly was not genuine in anything he practised, especially medicine!

BUT he was very genuine in wanting to do a job of murder on a famous police officer in New York City. But he was at the same time very stingy about the costs involved in the assassination of targeted Police Commander Robert Stewart. He certainly did not want to be left out of pocket through his scheme and scam of trying to save his brother in his own mind's delusion from spending the rest of his life in prison. So, Steven Archer wanted to enlist the cooperation of many other corrupt medical practitioners within New York, which comprised of other psychiatrists, GP doctors and even hospital surgeons and nurses and even bent psychologists, to split evenly the expenditure damage and the payment share of the expense to hire the most professional hitman to kill and assassinate Commander Robert Stewart.

Robert Stewart's investigation into exposing medical corruption in New York City was rapidly proving a justice-serving success for him and the New York City Police Department! And even to his painful admission, Robert Stewart had to carefully examine the words Domenico Armando used in reference to the medical profession; the accusations he made against so-called medical professionals; when Domenico Armando accused doctors of being corrupt, causing the death of his son George. Robert Stewart, what with, through the evidence established against the corruption of medical practitioners in New York so far at present - and established rather quickly at that, had him-the police Commander Robert Stewart for the first time in his police profession being forced to agree with a sick maniac called Domenico Armando, that established without a doubt, medical corruption in the city of New York was indeed proven to exist at epidemic proportions. But there was one slight difference between Robert Stewart's methods and Domenico Armando's methods. Robert Stewart wanted to arrest all the corrupt medical practitioner sons of bitches. Domenico Armando wanted to use violence and blow their heads off at the same time as plotting and scheming murderous bloodbaths following the utilisation of his deadly weapons, as well as exposing such criminal medical doctors and criminal medical nurses throughout the city to atomic and nuclear explosive warfare excruciating mass murders!

It was a question of who was going to eliminate the criminal medical practitioners and criminal nurses first? Was Robert Stewart going to be able to arrest all of them before Domenico Armando had in fact used violence to slaughter them? Or was the monstrously evil Domenico Armando going to in fact unleash all hell inflicted horrendous deaths upon the medical criminals in titanic proportions, before his rival Commander Robert Stewart outlived his exhaustive investigations to identify and prosecute every medical practitioner fraud and criminal thief in the entire city and state of New York?

CHAPTER 3

It was only 24 hours later, when Robert Stewart identified a sort of group gathering meeting being called between Steven Archer and 47 corrupt medical practitioners, including several nurses, with five additional psychologists, totalling a number of 52 people that was summoned at his Queens mansion house after working hours at midnight, to discuss the murder, the equal funding of the murder and the appointment of the specific hitman to do the murder against Commander Robert Stewart.

The meeting of these Criminal Minds comprising of medical practitioners and medical nurses, with the addition of bent and corrupt psychologists added to the mix across the New York area, was recorded by the police utilising perfect and dynamic surveillance strategies and necessary equipment, for evidence gathering purposes for a court of law. And the evidence established by the police so far, led by Commander Robert Stewart into the investigation of medical corruption throughout New York was remarkably effective. Robert Stewart watched these medical practitioner criminals and their aiding and abetting fiendish nurses and psychologists bury themselves alive. By their own admissions and conspired actions to commit murder against a cop, they, most certainly and rather swiftly, if not rapidly, dug their own graves systematically one by one and holistically altogether! It was the workings of true perfection by Robert Stewart and his law enforcement comrades witnessing this entire sordid spectacle of criminal doctors, wicked nurses and diabolical psychologists, not only admitting to killing their patients, but also admitting amongst themselves, to wanting to equally split the difference and equally fund the hiring of a specific hitman to do them a justice or a warped justice in the eyes of the justice system, which defined the death and demise of reputed police official, who went by the title of Commander Robert Stewart!

Doctors of all various ethnicities and age and backgrounds attended Psychiatrist Steven Archer's house this evening for the crucial mass gathering, beginning at midnight, to discuss their plans to equally fund the hitman to kill and assassinate Commander Robert Stewart. Doctors comprised of young and old Asian, Indian, American, Australian, French and Egyptian descent. And the nurses were of similar backgrounds and ethnicities, comprising of young and old age groups. They too participated in wanting to witness the demise of the one cop who could expose their grand corruption schemes and scams of murder against their patients through misdiagnoses, and the administering of incorrect medications, which resulted in the deterioration and thus deaths of masses of sick patients throughout the course of their careers. The psychologists in attendance were all of American descent with various age groups. And now they all discussed outside their operating medical duty hours to commit murder and fund the murder of the one cop they all agreed, was a threat to exposing their corruption and ending their well-paid jobs they received and got away with performing negligently and corruptly for the lifetime generation they practised their medical careers in New York. Some doctors were educated in overseas countries and then had to educate themselves in America in order to be recognised as the United States of America's legitimate practising practitioners of medicine and medical nurses. They had to register and go to university to achieve qualifications in the United States of America, so they could be recognised at the same time they obtained permanent residency to live in the United States of America and practise medicine inside the country legitimately. But behind the scenes, and behind their so-called qualifications, they were not practising medicine legitimately. They were practising medicine negligently and criminally. They were all guilty of being bankrupt in possessing any morals and ethics to care for their patients and treat them accordingly in a correct medical fashion, full stop. But they instead manipulated their status and manipulated their medical practises and medical duties to in fact inflict much harm, suffering and death upon their patients. And up until now, they had all gotten away with it... That was until Robert Stewart mounted his investigative crackdown on medical corruption in the city - and vowed to put an end to their killing sprees against patients and, in the process, their united funding for his personal demise as a Commander of the New York City Police Department.

Robert Stewart was on a fervent campaign to end these criminals dead in their tracks. He wanted to end their existences of fraud, deception, manipulation - and close down their fake and phoney practises in which they practised medicine, which resulted in the calculated monetary gains by the accumulation of patient numbers, and the cold-and-calculated slaughters behind the scenes of their patients.

They got away with their negligence and wilful corruption from day one of beginning their medical careers in the city and country. And Robert Stewart was adamant to put an end to these walking horror stories.

Robert Stewart was adamant to put an end to these forms of human filth disguised as doctors and nurses in the city, who were intentionally collecting large sums of money from their patients, pretentiously offering them correct medical treatments, when in actuality they were misdiagnosing them through their ignorance and criminally immoral beings, which resulted in hundreds, thousands and even millions of patients dying from otherwise curable conditions, had the doctors possessed the correct knowledge and the correct moral compass to treat their patients correctly!

But Robert Stewart unfortunately had to concur with his worst enemy's assessment that medical corruption did indeed result in the death of his son George the Great. Such carelessly sadistic and uncaring fraudulent thieving doctors were truly responsible for the death of Domenico Armando's son George! These doctors had killed their patients and doctors of the like certainly killed Domenico Armando's son. They were all responsible for his death. Robert Stewart had to admit (even if the admission was painful), that Domenico Armando this time was not talking shit. Domenico Armando was dead on the money. **He was spot on when he said that doctors were slobs and terrorists, full stop!** And the nurses were also much proven to match that horrendous description of their doctor practising counterparts.

Robert Stewart felt the anger building inside of him. He felt the rage building up in every fibre of his being. On the surface, his emotions seemed calm. But from the evidence accumulated against these medical terrorists and mass killers so far, and quite rapidly, Robert Stewart most certainly wanted to nail each and every one of them to the wall. Robert Stewart wanted to send all of them hanging inside their fucking cells. These culprits, these ratbags, these filthy pieces of human filth and trash disguised as doctors and nurses seriously deserved what was coming to them, Robert Stewart considered in his sudden raging mind and out loud to his police compatriots, who were witnessing the very discreet and elaborate surveillance operation into this medical corruption now unearthed in great detail inside Psychiatrist Steven Archer's Mansion House at present in the darkness. And it was in the darkness where these heinous criminals disguised as doctors and nurses were discussing their plans for murder. They were discussing their sick plans and admissions of patient deaths for the sole purpose of monetary gains. And now they were desperately discussing their plans to kill Robert Stewart, a professional cop in the dark. It was in the dark, in the shadows, without witnesses, so they thought, they were discussing all of this. But they were unaware that Robert Stewart behind the scenes was shining a light on their dark room conspiracies in the dead of night. Robert Stewart was shining a light of beautifully poetic exposure into their sick, cold-and-calculated mass murderous crimes against their patients, motivated by greed, selfishness, carelessness and a thirst for amassing large sums of money in the process.

Robert Stewart also exposed their sick plans and their sick schemes to equally fund his death, by splitting the difference of monetary sums of cash to fund a hitman, a specific hitman they would discuss also in the darkness to perform the deed, the gross misdeed. It was also a heinous crime of equally deadly proportions to kill a cop. But not just one ordinary cop. They in fact intended to assassinate and plot and scheme the conspired death and horrendous conspiracy to put

Commander Robert Stewart into the grave at that very moment! And this gathering of evil people with evil intentions, spouting evil wicked words out of their mouths, was the crux of their murderous and horrendous discussions, which uncovered and exposed into the light the true words of medical corruption being thrown their way, towards law enforcement to solemnly witness!

When these medical doctors and medical creeps were labelled as 'slobs and terrorists' by Domenico Armando, Robert Stewart considered that his archenemy rival's words were most certainly no lie, period! Because the words from his monster enemy Domenico Armando were in fact spot on and accurate in their assessments. And Robert Stewart concluded right now that no truer words were ever spoken in reference to, calling the criminal identified and exposed medical doctors and medical thugs as slobs and terrorists! Robert Stewart had to admit to his police comrades involved in the investigation against medical corruption in New York at present, that these horrible people, these horrible doctors and horrible nurses much proven by the police investigation to be human filth, could most certainly and most accurately be defined as slobs and terrorists. Therefore, Robert Stewart wanted them off the streets. Robert Stewart wanted them stripped of their licences to practise medicine completely. Robert Stewart wanted them behind bars immediately, full stop! Robert Stewart wanted them sent packing from this Steven Archer mansion and sent to their well-deserved death penalties. Robert Stewart wanted to see them literally hanged for their indescribable sick maniacal lunacies, of mass murderous crimes against their patients, and the sick maniacal horrendously terrible crime they conspired right now to have him, a police officer, murdered on top of all the deaths they had already been responsible for committing inside their medical practises, since the beginning of their horrible careers commencing in the United States of America! The evidence kept mounting against them. Robert Stewart watched and waited for these ratbags, swine and filthy evildoers to literally talk their way into the very graves they sent their patients - and unanimously conspired to send Robert Stewart inside at this very moment in time!

CHAPTER 4

And these were the horrendous words Robert Stewart overheard such disgusting despicable deplorables, who were an insult to the medical profession, being discussed inside Psychiatrist Steven Archer's mansion home at present.

"Robert Stewart must be terminated at once!" Were the words of a middle-aged Chinese doctor.

"Yes. That bloody cop Robert Stewart knows too much. We cannot afford to have him unearth all our dirty activities and put us in prison like he put our friend Psychiatrist Steven Archer's brother Elliot Archer behind bars, waiting to be sentenced to life. We cannot take the risk of Robert Stewart remaining among the living any longer. We must deal with him by giving him a taste of his own medicine we will, we must prescribe to him. Yes. We must prescribe to him a deadly poison. We must administer to him something very lethal, to stop him, once and for all and for good! The perfect prescription he must be given that will end his life and end the threat his existence constantly poses against us!" Were the words of a 65-year-old Indian doctor.

"Oh, if only it was as simple to kill him as it was one of our patients. Oh, oh, oh, oh… If only, if only, if only… If only we could kill Robert Stewart as simply as we dispose of our patients. Because let me tell everyone inside this room right now, Robert Stewart's death would certainly, most definitely would solve so many problems! In fact, he is so dangerous to all his targets, that I predict his death would solve all our problems immediately, on the spot and forever!" Said a pudgy 55-year-old nurse with a diabolical pig face and beefy red cheeks and very diabolically mean eyes. One glance at her would describe an insult of a woman who was both ugly on the inside and ugly on the outside. In fact, if all women were like her, it would most certainly drive all men to permanent singlehood and sexless existences!

"I personally would like to drive a knife through his stomach. I believe in the tradition of terrorism and extremism when it comes to disposing of such an enemy threat as this fool who calls himself Commander Robert Stewart!" Were the words of an Egyptian middle-aged doctor.

"I'm very tight with my money, for hell's sake. If only there was a cheaper way to kill Robert Stewart. I really hate spending a lot of money on one area. Perhaps I am a miser, but because there is no other way, I am very willing to this time spend a large sum of money in equal share with the rest of you gathered here inside this living room of Steven Archer's mansion to fund the death, the necessary death of this horrible commander of police, whose name is Robert Stewart!" Said a French doctor in his early thirties, with an almost resembling breathless weak husky voice, matching an unmasculine slender body in his cowardly worded delivery, to plot the death of a famous police officer behind that famous police officer's back!

Robert Stewart had the evidence to convict all of them and sentence them to the maximum penalty for their mass murderous crimes - and the conspiracy to commit murder against him as a New York Police official. Robert Stewart got them good. He had amassed the evidence so far that would most certainly result in their downfalls and destructions on the spot immediately. But for now, Robert Stewart halted on their arrests, PERIOD! Robert Stewart's intent, his entire approach, was calculated, cunning, dangerously clever and extremely prudent. Robert Stewart would eventually lead his police armies inside the mansion to arrest all the criminal doctors and criminal nurses, with the criminal psychologists, but for now, his instincts told him to wait and let them keep talking. Let them keep digging their graves. It was as if Robert was using precise strategy and ingenious investigative techniques to let them self-incriminate themselves in great detail, to uncover and unveil every aspect of their criminal lives as medical monsters living and practising in the heart of New York! So, Robert let them keep talking for now. Robert wanted them to spill their guts and expose every detail of their sick insane crimes they were committing throughout their entire medical professional careers; careers they were unjustly permitted to practise within the four walls of New York's heartland!

The criminal doctors and criminal nurses throughout their discussions had redefined the words **'medical corruption'.** And Robert Stewart was again forced to agree that when Domenico Armando called the doctors crooks, his assessment was wholeheartedly truthful.

The doctors and nurses were guilty of committing medical corruption via their dishonest practises within the United States of America's healthcare system! They would even resort to accepting bribes to commit fraud via incorrect patients' diagnoses and the practise of prescribing incorrect medications for such incorrect diagnoses. They would misuse their resources available to them to extract more money from their patients by giving them unnecessary blood tests and unnecessary X-rays, than otherwise needed. Which were not needed at all! So, the patients paid more. And if any results showed on the X-rays in additional annual checkup visits, they would even resort to embellishing results and hiding possible lethal conditions, so that the mistreatment and deaths of their patients would most certainly surface at a more rapid time frame, than if such patients were able to receive the correct medical treatments otherwise. Ordinarily, X-rays and blood tests may be ordered annually. But these criminal doctors and criminal nurses were ordering their patients to undergo these very expensive treatments on extremely frequent, and sometimes monthly basis, which was unnecessary. And this was what was defined as the misuse of resources and the short-changing of patients' monetary costs, which certainly undermined public trust on all levels!

And the concealment of truthful health conditions by (trusted???) doctors posed significant and lethal health risks on to the patients as well as incorrect medications, via the administering of unsafe treatments and the monstrous denial of proper access to health care. These were all the discussions that Robert Stewart had uncovered throughout his current superiorly masterful investigations against medical corruption in the city. What these criminal doctors and criminal nurses were committing had surely resulted in the unnecessary deaths of masses of their patients even in a short space of time! And Robert Stewart kept watching and kept waiting for them to further expose the true hell out of their very existences. Robert Stewart didn't just want them in prison. He wanted to see each and every one of them literally burnt at the stake, with all the ammunition he defined as evidence accumulated against every filthy maggot male and female one of them; those disgusting and disgraceful insults to the medical community of the United States of America!

The doctors and nurses had communicated everything, revealing all their crimes and hidden emotions now revealed out in the open amongst themselves. They also disclosed how they felt exposed in Robert Stewart's presence. "This guy is a fucking human lie detector!" A 57-year-old American doctor insisted. And then the rest of them gathered inside the mansion's living room area would shout and scream in crazy-insane agreement amongst each other. They were most certainly desperate to fund Robert Stewart's death right now, thinking that that one death would save them from their own demises, his one life would otherwise create against them all!

They all viewed Robert as a very dangerous man. His electric gaze was defined as sending chills down their spines. They considered that Robert Stewart would stare them down without any words spoken for a period of time, and just through his very intimidating gaze, he would unearth all their hideous secrets and send them to death row before they could prescribe their next deadly poison to their next victim patient! And/or prescribe such deadly poison to Robert Stewart himself.

The corrupt doctors and the corrupt nurses, mixed together with the heinous psychologists, did not only fear Robert Stewart's words, but they also feared his silence. They feared what he could see when he looked at them even with no words spoken! They were experiencing a quiet terror at first and then they vocalised their admissions of horror by Robert Stewart's presence remaining among the living, period!!! They were admitting to each other out loud that Robert Stewart had to go. And the one 65-year-old Indian doctor amongst them had spoken words that every doctor, nurse and psychologist present inside the room were thinking in agreement. "That menacing and threatening cop has to die right along with his death stare of us all!" Shouted the 65-year-old Indian Doctor before his gathered audience base of unethically bankrupt and immorally insane medical colleagues and friends. They hinted in agreement such words, "Exactly. We know, we know, we bloody know!" Before the Indian doctor continued his lunatic rant: "that Robert Stewart cop is a maniac. He sees things that others do not see. He notices things that others can never notice and/or simply ignore. We must all consider that Robert is too dangerous to be alive any longer! Robert Stewart will surely uncover all our weaknesses. He will surely expose all our lies and unmask all our fake and phoney facades of murder, mass murder and conspiracy to commit more murder not only inside our medical practises, but against him-Robert Stewart himself. Just by Robert Stewart remaining among the living, we all feel naked and exposed. I must admit before you all, my esteemed friends and colleagues, that we cannot hide nothing from Robert Stewart, period!!! Maybe we can hide things from the rest of the damn cops in this city, but, but, but... not Robert Stewart.

"Even right now, when we are talking in the darkness of the night amongst ourselves, hidden inside this mansion, we must become paranoid that Robert is around... is around somewhere... And he can see us, all of us somehow... He could see us and unearth our discussions. And even unravel our secret thoughts, full stop!!!

"This fucking son of a bitch crafty devil of a cop called Commander Robert Stewart, has most certainly instilled nasty negative thoughts in our minds. He has instilled this paranoia, and he has made 'us all' fearful! And I am sure I am speaking for all of us, not just for myself, when I insist that this fear instilled in our minds, hearts and souls by this one damn cop Commander Robert Stewart, has produced various other emotions as a consequence of this fear! Our fear has also made us angry. And a mixture of fear and anger will have us all risk everything, our entire existences, by plotting and scheming and pooling our monetary funds together, and amalgamate our resources, to resolve that fear and paranoia and anger we are now currently feeling at present, by agreeing, all agreeing to kill Robert Stewart at once, on the double, immediately - and with no fucking hesitation!

"That fucking cop Robert Stewart sees everything. We have all cried out loud together all at once - and more than once - by the very repercussions of Robert Stewart's damning presence served against us. I believe he can even read our minds. And I know what we are all thinking. We have all come to the same consensus. Every diabolical thought we currently share in common concerning this diabolical threat against us Robert Stewart must be put to productive use. We must put those shared negative thoughts of ours into murderous actions, full stop!!! Therefore, and henceforth at once, Robert Stewart must die before he broadcasts his suspicions of what he sees when he thinks of us to the wider community of police working with him! I truly believe the police masses are ignorant! But it is Robert Stewart who is feeding them stories about us. It is Robert Stewart who is educating his police colleagues in the entire city and state of New York. This act of rebellion against us by this one fucking cop Robert Stewart must be dealt with immediately! We cannot... We cannot... We fucking cannot tolerate this enemy serving against us called Robert Stewart for one second longer! We must kill Robert while those thoughts are embedded in his skull, and in his mind alone, before he broadcasts them to the entire New York Police Force." Indicated rather desperately the 65-year-old Indian Doctor ferociously and ruthlessly. And many of his evil and wicked colleagues gathered around him at this present moment in time, would cry out loud such fearful thoughts of that one police commander named Robert Stewart. But they all feared Robert Stewart. They all feared the mysterious power, the magical psychic power of this one threatening fiend in their minds whose name was Commander Robert Stewart! The power Robert exuded by instilling fear, doubt and paranoia throughout the depths of their minds, sent them on a wild campaign and into drafting a hideously master maniacal blueprint plan of plotting and scheming this one cop's conspired, but in their minds, necessary murder at this very moment!

They all feared Robert Stewart's razor focus. They all feared his awareness and his unrelenting alignment that other ordinary cops could never match, even in their wildest hallucinations and vivid nightmares! Because right now, in their minds, Robert Stewart was a man who could crumble the walls of buildings these criminals were situated inside. He had vision and perception skills that could see through very thick brick walls. He could unearth every detail, every sordid detail of their lives existences. Nothing escaped him. Nothing was beyond reproach when it came to Robert Stewart's much feared see-through-lead eyesight, and mind-reading and mind-exposing magical abilities, of his very sharp and resilient mindset against criminals as these in general! No lie remained a secret with Robert Stewart! No so-called foolproof plan would even remain hidden! As long as Robert Stewart was alive, they considered their entire sordid lives dirty works just a hair from being exposed!

Robert Stewart did not need to say anything. He would just watch and wait and let his targets slip themselves into their own graves. And that was what these criminal doctors, criminal psychologists and criminal nurses felt right now. Such dreadful horrendous fear of exposure!

Robert Stewart's entire existence became a spooky Horror Story to them. They feared his life and they were terrified of every breath it consumed, which meant one more threat against them. The ageing old Indian doctor continued his lunacy and masterfully flawed, yet domineering, but still maniacal word delivery before his ruthlessly corrupt friends and colleagues gathered around him this evening (or dark early morning), inside Steven Archer's living room mansion. "That son of a bitch irritating cop Commander Robert Stewart notices things that escapes everyone else," the dumb son of a bitch Indian doctor barked in antagonistic disdain. The Indian Doctor had stolen the show and was unstoppable, as he resumed the role of autocratic speaker at present before his much fucked-in-the-head audience base gathered before him. The Indian doctor continued his aggressive and bossy high-and-mighty self-incriminating words, **"Subtle. Yes, that truly defines Robert Stewart's style, his methods, and the blueprint in how that sneaky conniving cunning sly cop operates. Very subtle.** But he crawls and slithers throughout New York City much like an attacking crocodile with sharp teeth, silently, before he pounces on his targets and swallows them up in a checkmate victory. **He has to die before he checkmates all of us!** With every gaze from his sneaky eyes, and with every observation, we cannot keep any secrets from him, period!!! We cannot talk out loud. We cannot even think out loud to ourselves. That son of a bitch cop Robert Stewart will telepathically pick up our thoughts before we even implement our plans into actions. He cannot be left to his own devices any longer. Every second that crocodile is left breathing and slithering through this city, he will uncover more secrets against us, just through reading our minds. Or glancing his gaze, using his tyrannical X-ray vision targeted our way! He simply has to go! As long as Robert Stewart is alive, we have no control over our physical actions. As long as Robert Stewart is alive, he will continue to dominate our physical realities! And just by his very existence alone, he sabotages our emotions. From stable, we have become paranoid. From secure, we are now succumbed to being paralysed in fear. No, no, no, no, no... No more I say! No more must this continue any longer! His life must not be permitted for one second longer.

"That bastard Robert Stewart doesn't need to say a word, full stop! All he has to do, is just throw a silent stare in our direction, and he will unearth all our secrets. Is this the fear we want to live for the rest of our lives?

"I hate Robert Stewart because he has turned my confidence into dread. Whilst we were setting traps for our patients, Robert Stewart no doubt is setting traps for us as well at the same time. I hate Robert Stewart because he offers us resistance. I hate Robert Stewart because even in his physical absence, he is plotting our downfalls. I hate Robert Stewart because he has the power to make all our plans and schemes irrelevant, obsolete and turned to dust! I hate Robert Stewart because he can win a war against us even before he engages. I hate Robert Stewart because he can attack us even in the darkness, without any of us seeing his presence among us! Even before we see him and he vocalises his verbal disagreement and arguments with us, he can still break us, period! And I hate Robert Stewart, because he is able to outwit us and outsmart us and outmanoeuvre us, even when we cannot see him and what he is doing against us! Even when we cannot see him as an opponent, he can defeat us in a masterstroke just by sheer willpower and uncanny perception! I hate Robert Stewart because of his abilities to do that! Even when he is not among us, as we are counting the most points we have scored against all our former patients' deaths, Robert Stewart is hiding someplace, ending the scoreboard on his unseen chessboard, as he closes in, in silence, surreptitiously, officially towards our defeats and checkmates! Because of that, I hate Robert Stewart!

"I despise Robert Stewart! I hate Robert Stewart because he never underestimates anybody. And because of what he sees every time he looks at us, even from a distance many, many miles away, after what he sees, he makes criminals like us fear him! Robert Stewart has the uncanny ability to see the patterns in our criminal behaviours that all other people miss. And he plans to expose all our power plays even when we cannot see him doing it. He can uncover all our manipulations just by strategy! And you know how cunning this horrible cop truly is? He will never interrupt us in our plans. He will let us keep talking. He will let us keep exposing ourselves throughout our criminal actions and criminal behaviours. He will sit there waiting for us to bloody our hands fully - and then like a crocodile slithering through the streets of New York City, he will have each and every one of us surprised, by bursting in our homes and attacking us with his sharp teeth. And that is how he destroys all criminals.

"And so, I hate Robert Stewart because we cannot hide anything from him! Robert Stewart plays very diabolical games with people like us. He makes us feel confident, calm and secure to commit our crimes, when he zeroes in on our defences and exposes all out hidden secrets. And then he destroys us through such exposures, one by one and altogether! I hate Robert Stewart because of his ability to do that!

"Robert Stewart is a psychopath of titanic proportions against criminals like us! And whilst we feel that we are mapping out our victories against the law, Robert Stewart is silently and ruthlessly, like a snake in the grass, mapping out the complete destructions of all of us. I hate Robert Stewart because of that!

"Robert Stewart just sits there quietly plotting against us. He never rushes himself. He never rushes in against us! He sits there quietly and observes us digging our own graves. And then he makes his move against us, once he has accumulated every piece of information and evidence of our exposures. But first waiting for us to keep talking and revealing our hands, through self-incriminating words and deeds. I hate Robert Stewart because of his ability to do that! Robert Stewart sits there like a strategic monster - and then he strikes at his targets before they have any moves left in them. He strikes when there is nothing left on the chessboard for his targeted enemies to use against him! I hate Robert Stewart for that.

"I hate Robert Stewart because as we prepare for war, he has already made his move to surround us, outnumber us, and shoot us down dead, before we can even enter the battlefield! The truth is, us criminals emotionally want power over Robert Stewart. But he defeats us every time with clarity. How can we defeat a man like that? That is why I will fund every last penny I have in my bank account, to invest in his immediate death and destruction.

"I hate Robert Stewart, because with a click of his fingers, he can make us lose relevance in every aspect of our lives, both personally and professionally! Full stop! Period! As we feel important, he can diminish us with a single blink of his eyes. I hate Robert Stewart because of that. Robert Stewart shows us no anger, no emotion, no resistance. He lets us do all the talking and the self-incriminating and the exposing of ourselves. All the while, he waits and watches, listens and plots in the dark all our downfalls, before we can strike and succeed in our plans against him. That's why I hate Robert Stewart! He only shows composure whilst keeping his nasty attacks against us well concealed and well hidden. I hate Robert Stewart for that. And I hate Robert Stewart because he understands all our true colours early. He sees what we are, and he sees through all our pretensions and well-conceived plots and schemes and behavioural patterns and character flaws in silence. He sees through all our con artistry! He knows we are all fake and phoney ignorant fucking useless, worthless murdering shits! But he lets us think otherwise. He lets us think that we have the upper hand and we are winning. His intention is to let us climb the mountain very high, before he approaches us and checkmates us; so, the fall is all the more greater, harder and more painful, when he finally decides to pull the rug from under us - and leads us to our downfalls and destructions, in one masterstroke after the other! That is how he tricks us. He likes to play games with us! He lets us think that we are deceiving everybody, but Robert Stewart is the greatest deceiver of them all. He deceives us so naturally, so cleverly, that we cannot even see that he will destroy us invisibly, when we think we have gotten away with all our crimes!

"He knows what we are without telling us that he knows. He just listens and observes with complete unemotional clarity, before he makes his move against us! I hate Robert Stewart because of his ability to do that!

"This…this is how cunning that bastard cop Robert Stewart is. Listen, listen, listen, fucking listen to this goddamn fucking story. He just sits there silent and invisible, letting us roll the dice to our fates and destinies of destruction. He plays games and dirty tricks with us, letting us feel confident in our sick plans and evil schemes. He just remains invisible, watching us, watching our every move... And all the while he is there waiting for us, yes, waiting for us to expose ourselves and our plans. He is there watching and listening invisibly, without us knowing about it, saying nothing. Just sitting there, observing us. And then, when we least expect it, he moves in for the kill, with our jaws hung down from our faces, in the greatest of surprise. I hate Robert Stewart for that.

"I hate Robert Stewart for his innate ability to make us all feel small without even any effort. I hate Robert Stewart because through his calm and calculated approach, he uncovers all our chaos. He sees through all our mayhem before our plans are ever cast forward! Robert Stewart doesn't expose our tactics early. He simply waits for us to talk ourselves into the grave he has already dug for each and every one of us in advance! His cold calculated manipulative silence dismantles in one second what takes us lifetimes to build. Who among us cannot hate Robert Stewart for that?

"I hate Robert Stewart for making us feel confident and clever before his awareness and perception swallows us up via his premeditated trap - and sends us into the fire below our feet.

"I hate Robert Stewart because he never speaks revenge against us. He shows us his revenge by his masterful actions which takes us all by surprise! I hate Robert Stewart because he can take away all our freedoms before we have all learned how to spell the word! I hate Robert Stewart because just as we are plotting his downfall as we speak, I know he is plotting a diabolical scheme for our complete and absolute destructions!

"I hate Robert Stewart because his absence forces us to have a false sense of security, exposing ourselves through our actions and our words, before he surprisingly makes his move, that sends all of us into our graves. Robert Stewart does not show us his hand. No words, no intentions, no prior warning. He just lets us speak our true words and lets us plot our sickest actions, when he hangs us all after we first expose ourselves. Let us not kid ourselves. Robert Stewart has defeated us the moment he decided to remain absent and let us send ourselves to his electric chair! He gives no explanations, only invisibility. He does not threaten us, only lets us threaten our own existences through what we say and what we do.

"I hate Robert Stewart because he gives us nothing to go on. He doesn't approach us and tell us that he suspects us. No, fucking no. He never does that. He suspects us silently and plots our funerals invisibly. And that is how he always wins cleanly against sickos like us.

"I want to ask everyone here a very important question about this cop Commander Robert Stewart. Where are his scars? Where are his battle scars? I see none, because that sonofabitch Robert Stewart is a master at disposing of his targets, by simply letting those targets dispose of themselves. He simply just moves in to pick up the pieces and clean up the debris that we have already created amongst ourselves! He doesn't flaunt his trophies, his medals, his promotions. No. Fucking no. He is too much of a trickster for that. Robert Stewart handles us like the horse manure he truly believes we are. He acts quiet. He fools and fakes out the entire world of scumbags and low lives, before he moves in and exposes us via our own sick plans.

"But the truth is, Robert Stewart is a man who thrives on conflict. He survives only on conflict. As we want to see him crack, he remains invisible wanting the same thing for us. And he always succeeds in cracking us criminals before us criminals can ever crack one line on his forehead. That is how dangerous that cop Robert Stewart is, full stop! And that is why I hate him so much for his ability to do what no man can do. And his bloody fucking uncanny ability to make successful people like us crumble down into the ground in failure and despair, with no warning, no words, only one final checkmate action that compromises all our safeties - and lands us into one destined cemetery he has waiting for us, prearranged, no doubt, by his cold calculated invisible destructive hands. Does everyone here hate Robert Stewart for that? I certainly do. I hate Robert Stewart because he never gives us criminals the satisfaction of seeing our plans against him work. You know our plans for his murder. He lets us criminals waste a lot of time, a lot of effort and a lot of money investing in his destruction before he moves against us. Just like I hinted before. He gives us a false sense of security by letting us climb to the top of our crimes, before pulling the rug from right under our feet and sends us crashing down all the more painfully. And it's more painful to let us climb higher, thinking we're getting away with everything, than if he doesn't let us climb so high, before getting us. It is very painful to climb very high and fall all the way to the ground, than if you have never climbed high before and you fall. That is how cunning and devious, clever and dangerous Commander Robert Stewart is.

"He remains invisible. He keeps quiet. He watches us in silence. He lets us establish a false sense of security and a false sense of

47

confidence, before he moves in for our kill, period! And his method of operation and his final checkmate move against us is all the more painful by such hideous destructive strategic manipulative tactics he always has in the works against us criminals! I hate Robert Stewart because of all of that!

"Robert Stewart doesn't ruin our game early. He lets us play the game. He lets us think we're winning. And then, then, with no effort whatsoever, he flips the game over, replaces the table with his own board game, and forces us to play his chess game. Forcing us to lose our freedoms and our very lives through his own diabolically calculated hidden strategy he planned against us all along and masterfully invisibly! I hate Robert Stewart because of that!

"He checkmates us before we even think of contemplating a rematch. He has defeated all of us before we even think that we have started the game! Because he sits back quietly and lets us make our weak moves, before he makes his final strongest move to obliterate us before we even learn the rules of the game. The rules of the game that he has mastered and the rules of the game that he forces us to play, using blind strokes and invisible instructions. And that is why he always comes out the winner! He truly designed the game to always make us lose. I hate Robert Stewart because of that.

"And you want to know what really enrages manipulators like us? It is the invisible ghost called Robert Stewart manipulating our downfalls in more diabolical proportions behind the scenes. I hate Robert Stewart because he never confronts us and exposes his intentions against us publicly. He looks at us in the shadows and plots our downfalls in secret. He lets us sit alone with what we have planned, words and actions. And then he makes his move to arrest us all. I hate Robert Stewart because he never warns us criminals that he is so smart. He never tells us that he sees all and knows all about us, even from a great distance! He just lets us think that we are smarter than him before he makes his final move to point his gun at us and blow our heads off, sending us head and body into kingdom come. He doesn't confront us because he thinks of us as worthless beings.

"Robert Stewart knows it would be a privilege for him to confront us. But he insults us by only talking to us when he wishes to either use violence or his handcuffs against us or both! He lets us play time with false confidence. And there is nothing, no better strategy for him to attack his opponents, than to allow them to gain an unwise perception of themselves built on false confidence. I hate Robert Stewart because he loves us to compete with him, when he already dictated the instruction manual of our downfalls, before we ever could think that we were competition to him. I hate Robert Stewart because he never loses patience and time does not influence his decisions when it comes to destroying us criminals. I hate Robert Stewart because he peaks when he is subjected to hellish pressure, the same pressure that would make the rest of us crumble in defeat into the ground and succumb to death itself.

"Robert Stewart utilises patience in his police profession. Because time and patience is how we expose ourselves to him. He is very cunning, very clever, very dangerous and very manipulative.

"Robert Stewart is a psychological war master! He is a psychological war general! He is mentally and physically a wartime combative warrior. He wins by attrition and cunning. He is a master manipulator, a magician, a wizard, perhaps a sorcerer! He is very analytical, very observant. He is composed whilst his targets unravel! No one can get one over on him! First, he breaks people mentally, whilst making them think they're on top of the world. And then he charges inside their homes and checkmates them physically, by opening fire his weapons of war against his targeted enemies, until all his threats are dead. Robert Stewart's abilities are limitless! His punishment against his targets is unmatched!!And that is why he always wins! So, I say let us kill him now, so he can never win against us again!"

And the applause to the doctor's words by the surrounding crowd resonated for many moments to come.

CHAPTER 5

Robert Stewart watched and listened to the criminal doctors, nurses and psychologists plotting his downfall from his safe inconspicuous distance inside his police unmarked nondescript and unidentifiable, white-coloured surveillance van parked close by but not too close.

Robert Stewart had perfect hidden cameras and hidden listening devices known as bugs planted inside Steven Archer's mansion, as he watched and listened to the evil doctors, wicked nurses and deranged psychologists plot their black ends by conspiring his downfall.

The horrendously wicked and foolish medical practitioners thought they could outsmart fate by getting away with their numerously immense crimes of mass murder against their unknowing patients over the years - and now in addition to all of that, plotting to kill Robert, by joining forces unanimously and equally contributing their monetary savings into a specifically appointed hitman to assassinate Commander Robert Stewart.

Robert Stewart was dissecting all their words as a forensic pathologist dissected a corpse, by cutting it open inch by inch and examining every aspect of its head and body and determining cause of death and what evil disease or diseases lay inside its dead remains. Robert Stewart wanted proof, concrete undisputable proof of these medical workers wrongdoings. And he obtained that goal rather proficiently and masterfully. But Robert Stewart proved that patience in police work was a virtue. So, he waited until these people spoke themselves into an eternal death sentence. And Robert Stewart would not move in for the kill against them and had not ordered their arrests until he had accomplished just that and obtained every piece of information, every lead, every admission and every criminal murderous plot and scheme which spat out of their evil mouths, one by one and altogether. Their fates were now destined for destruction.

And the moment they also plotted together to kill a police officer, was also the very moment they signed the official papers for not only their downfalls, but for their sanctioned corpses to enter hell and burn deservedly for their hideous and monstrous crimes!

The ringleader among them who appointed himself the mastermind to the crime of assassinating Commander Robert Stewart was called Psychiatrist Steven Archer. Steven Archer was the one who decided amongst them the plan to pay a hitman equally to do just that, to terminate Robert Stewart.

These fake and phoney medical practitioners all had degrees, framed certificates and legal credentials to practise medicine in the United States of America. And they chose New York City to each open their practises, devising a scheme of murder, cruel manipulated murder of their patients for money, full stop! And now they also plotted the monstrous crime of killing a cop named Robert Stewart. Also, they admitted that after they left university, they knew nothing about how to treat sick patients, period. Some clever doctors studied additional medical books in the aftermath of leaving university in order to teach themselves proper skills and lessons in how to treat patients accordingly and solve problems. But not these reckless heinous individuals gathered inside Psychiatrist Steven Archer's mansion in the dead of night. No. Not these arseholes and creeps. Not at all. Instead, they used cunning and devious tactics to use their medical credentials to open the doors of their clinics to commit a legalised killing spree and killing sprees of their patients, after they snatched large sums of money from them. And the patients were in very bad shape to begin with. A lot of them had horrendous diseases and excruciatingly crippling medical conditions that needed urgent attention.

So, doctors as these gathered inside Steven Archer's house were instead treating the symptoms of their patients, whilst all the while worsening their problems. They misdiagnosed them out of ignorance and corruption and wilfully gave them incorrect medications, which would not only make their original health conditions worse, but cause new health conditions such as liver problems, kidney problems, heart problems, digestive problems, respiratory problems, mental confusion, mental disorientation - and a whole host of paralysing symptoms both mentally and physically, making a weak patient's condition even weaker. And behind the scenes, they-those evil and corrupt medical practitioners were enjoying themselves. To the patients' faces, they acted concerned. They pretended that their medications prescribed to their patients were correct medications, were properly prescribed medications designed to help them, even lying that such medications would heal them in time. And the patients were naturally not skilled in medical deception. Some of them had no life experience dealing with medical corruption.

And that was precisely what these cunning and manipulative corrupt and evil medical practitioners banked on. The corrupt doctors banked on their patients' ignorance in understanding that what they were being prescribed would never heal them, but in fact work to destroy them completely and send them into their graves!

Some criminal doctors took their patients as suckers. Acting concerned to their faces and behind their backs, plotted their downfalls and laughed at their destructions. And laughing when finally, their patients ended up dead, at the same time the doctors and nurses profited richly from the monetary gains from them before such deaths took place. It was a farce. It was a joke. It was a two-faced mask-wearing hypocritically diabolical catastrophe of medical corruption and evil medical negligence, deliberately directed against their inexperienced and unknowing patients, leading to the patient's demise and patients' demises (plural) and final ends as mass corpses inside a grave.

The doctors and the nurses were all laughing at the fact that they made huge sums of money for destroying their patients' lives!

And after prescribing such incorrect medications, the corrupt doctors and wicked nurses waited… They waited as horrible sinners in church waited for their turn inside the confessional with a delusional priest, pretending that the priest could wipe away their sins; the same evil crime was cast forward by wicked medical officials towards their patients. And such wicked medical officials constantly forced their patients to have too regular medical checkups and unnecessarily frequent blood tests and X-rays, which were costly medical procedures on an unnecessarily too frequent basis, designed by devious medical practitioners for the sole purpose of making huge sums of money from unknowing sucker patients.

And yes, yes indeed, the corrupt and wicked medical practitioners and repulsively unclean medical nurses waited. They surely waited for their incorrect diagnoses and incorrect medications to take their toll upon their patient victims. And they even looked forward to the patients' next appointments, to see that deterioration their destructive medications had caused to all their patients. And with much delight, they thrived behind the scenes as they watched their diminished patients' lives decrease further at their hands of horrible and incorrect medical procedures being bestowed upon those sick people who saw them as doctors and nurses. And once the patients became grossly ill from incorrect treatments, the GP doctors would refer the dying patients to criminal specialists. And such referrals to specialists had ensured that the specialists also made more money from the patients. The GPs already enjoyed having sick people's money splurged on them. The specialists who were in on the crimes in cahoots and in conspiracy with the GPs also prescribed incorrect medications, which caused sick, dying and those close to death patients to be further deteriorated in their health status, to the point of utter despair. And even at times paralysis.

Then once the specialists had deteriorated their patients' conditions further through negligence and wilful corruption, the specialists referred them to hospitals, where wicked doctors practising in hospitals and wicked nurses practising in hospitals had finished them off by simply drugging them to their complete deaths. And the doctors and the nurses inside hospitals were very expedient in their approaches of killing patients in wholesale massacre type speedy operations inside their public and private hospitals. They drugged them ferociously, which resulted in the patients eventually being unable to move their arms and legs, eat their food or even keep their eyes open from the toxically strong drugs they were constantly being given by doctors and nurses at all times of the day and night. The patients' death sentences proved very efficient inside such public and private hospitals run by corrupt doctors and corrupt nurses. The deterioration of those sick people was extremely rapid. The patients couldn't speak and they couldn't eat, could not walk and could not keep their eyes open, which caused them to die very quickly. And once in hospital, the doctors and the nurses insisted amongst themselves, that they wanted the patients to die quickly, because they needed their beds vacant for further patient victims to also be drugged and killed much the same way. But **NOT TO BE FORGOTTEN,** only to be drugged and killed after the patients paid them exorbitant monetary medical costs.

Medical corruption in New York City and proven across the entire United States of America, if not the entire world itself, through diabolically driven medical operations, which operated the same way across the globe was at epidemic proportions. In fact, it was fair, truthful and honest to say that corrupt doctors as a whole had been responsible for deliberately killing more people patients than every dictator in human history had been responsible for killing masses of people all combined. The doctors had proven to be the worst criminals to the human race than any living mass murderous tyrant and dictator in recent and distant history since the beginning of man and woman's creation!!!

What the corrupt doctors of the world had been responsible for committing was in fact defined as human devastation! Immoral, unethical, unmerciful and horrendously wicked evil human actions of animalistic destructive proportions! In fact, what these criminal doctors and criminal nurses were committing against their patients on a daily basis, warranted a form of Divine Justice to be thunder stormed down upon their heads so quickly, that their death certificates warranted for their crimes should be issued as rapidly as they all conspired in their very sick minds, to commit such horrendous atrocities against millions and millions and billions and billions of their patients over the generations!

And now the stupid and putrid doctors, nurses and psychologists gathered inside Psychiatrist Steven Archer's mansion in the dead of night began trembling. Their hands shaking. Their bodies trembling as a leaf in thought of the one cop who could destroy them, by uncovering their dirty little secrets and rotten scams, and sending them packing their bags into a life of confinement, if not certifiable deaths, in which they seriously deserved in Robert's eyes.

The doctors and nurses were scared that Robert Stewart would expose them and finally bring justice against them for their hideous crimes of patient mass murders what with at the same time, uncovering the plot against his life as a cop as well!

And those fiendish medical practitioners and medical practising nurses at present became extremely afraid, very scared of Robert Stewart's existence. Robert Stewart was seen as a big threat against them in exposing their crimes, and even terminating their existences the same way these horrendous medical officials were responsible for terminating countless of their patients' lives in the past! For a while these medical officials had been masking their fear of Robert Stewart. But upon the arrest of corrupt police officer Elliot Archer was thus confirmed by the very hands of Robert Stewart, the criminal doctors, criminal nurses and fiendish psychologists could no longer mask such fears of this one police official, who had a knack for seeing through dirt, as if such human replicated excrement species were as transparent as glass and even from a distance, the same as at close range, to Commander Robert Stewart.

The crux of the matter was as such: criminal doctors and criminal nurses felt very intimidated by Robert Stewart. Many of them never met him face to face. But they still were intimidated of him even from a distance. They were afraid of him as if they could instinctually sense that Robert at any time would zero in on them as a mind reader could read human thoughts.

The criminal doctors and criminal nurses knew they had everything bad to hide from Robert Stewart. Now they were pretending different scenarios within themselves to save face. They convinced themselves that they had to prove that they were still worthy of existing whilst Robert Stewart was still alive. But the fear and intimidation factor they felt was very real. Their paranoid minds and states of worry became uncontrollable. As long as Robert Stewart was breathing, he was extremely dangerous to them they proclaimed in their minds' unanimously, full stop! Thus, the united plan to hire a hitman and pay for that hitman equally to remove that one detrimental threat called Robert Stewart from their lives was sealed.

And in this instance as in many past situations during his police profession, Robert's proven supernatural intuition that was a gift had been responsible for saving his life in countless instances. This instance was not different. Upon Elliot Archer's arrest, Robert Stewart insisted to keep closer surveillance on the corrupt ex-cop inside his jail cell and monitor him closely, including all conversations with all visitors he would receive during his period of incarceration in the local jailhouse facility.

Robert Stewart's intuition had certainly saved his life by intuitively keeping tabs on Elliot Archer and his conversations he had with all his visitors. Which proved to him in real time, the conspiracy that Elliot Archer and his brother, the Psychiatrist Steven Archer had planned to kill him. And in turn, his instincts proved accurate once again, when he did not immediately order the arrest of Psychiatrist Steven Archer, but kept him on the loose for now under heavy surveillance, which was very discreet. And this brilliant surveillance and the monitoring of all his outside activities under discreet tight watch 24 hours of the day, had tremendously unravelled a greater plot, including many conspired doctors and nurses' plans, who also wanted to kill him, Robert Stewart himself.

Robert Stewart not only opened up the Pandora's Box to medical corruption holistically, but his intuition to keep Steven Archer on the loose for now, certainly saved Robert's life, when he uncovered the desperate numerous plots by many other medical frauds throughout New York to conspire to kill him. **And now Robert Stewart planned to get them all.** He planned to send them all to the furnace. He planned to have them all fry in that very dark and gruesome place of boiling hell!

Not only were these monster medical practising beings responsible for killing masses of their patients, but now they also were planning to kill a cop. Him. Robert Stewart!

Robert Stewart finally led the police to move in for the kill against the criminal doctors and criminal nurses at Steven Archer's mansion by 3:00 AM in the morning. The police wore bulletproof vests, because they knew the doctors and nurses were armed with guns and bullets. Not only were they paranoid of Robert Stewart, but they took precautions in the event that their paranoia of Robert Stewart's planned intentions against them, to bring them to justice was accurate.

Robert Stewart viewed the corrupt medical officials through his monitor screen showing off their artillery weapons they concealed inside their casual attires. Robert Stewart and the police stormed inside the Archer mansion, kicking down locked doors and cornering the mass group of perpetrators inside the mansion's prestigious living room area. The police had guns pointed at the doctors and nurses with five additional psychologists. The tallied number of criminal medical operators currently inside the Archer house at present became a number of 52. The doctors and nurses and psychologists were shocked at the police presence surrounding them. But because they were paranoid, they were hardly surprised, period! And in the confusion of their very sick minds acting out crazy fantasies of murderous crimes, they still thought they had a fighting chance to defeat Robert and his police comrades, so they attempted to pull out their weapons, ignoring Robert Stewart's words of surrender and be still. But they kept attempting to arm themselves with weapons in hands and point their pistols at the police - and rather unsuccessfully at that.

Robert Stewart ordered his army of police surrounding the perpetrator doctors and nurses and psychologists that moment to open fire. And the bloodbath against the medical practitioners and medical nurses, in addition to the psychologist frauds ensued as a result. The bullets fired by police at the total number of 52 armed enemy targets commenced, until the mission was complete and the threat was neutralised absolutely on all levels. The fired guns loaded with deadly bullets targeted against all the threatening evil doctors and evil nurses and wicked psychologists, kept shooting, until all enemy targets lay dead on the ground, no longer threatening lives of the present police, or the outside community, specifically their medical patients or any other law enforcement officer, comprising of the New York City constabulary, particularly meaning Commander Robert Stewart, also present inside the Archer mansion at this very moment, in which those now confirmed deceased medical sharks had previously and wilfully during their lively states, attempted to appoint a suitable candidate as hitman to do the job of the police commander's murder!

In Robert Stewart's mind, the deaths of those wicked doctors and evil nurses and vicious psychologists were not the end to his investigation against widespread medical corruption in the city of New York. His investigation against medical corruption was still in its infancy stages. But the uncovering of evidence against those dead medical perpetrators was indeed a major stepping stone and significant turning point into the right direction, in terms of exposing the extreme dangerous hazard that many doctors were perpetrating against their victim patients, costing those sick patients their health, their money and many of them their very lives!!!

CHAPTER 6

Domenico Armando wanted brutal revenge against the scum, the trashy lowlife pieces of shit medical creeps responsible for the death of his beloved son, George the Great!

Those doctors were the lowest of the low Domenico considered in himself. Those doctors did not deserve to remain alive for one second longer for what they do, the heinous crimes and torturous gutless scumbaggery of theft and physical and mental torment they inflict upon their patients on a daily basis. Domenico Armando planned his revenge right to the minutest detail. In a nutshell, he wanted those doctors dead! In his mind, in his black heart and in his dark soul, he sought no purpose to the world tolerating the existence of doctors any longer. The doctors cured no one. The doctors assisted no one. But they only stole their patients' money and inflicted cold-and-calculated horrible suffering onto their patients and the patients' loved ones, with no mercy, no compassion and no conscience whatsoever in their very sick beings, and even lack of backbones. Domenico Armando was planning his revenge in great detail. He planned to wipe out all the criminal doctors in New York City, and the United States of America, and would look to obliterate and terminate every criminal doctor from across the entire globe in many other countries. That was how angry and furious Domenico Armando was at the death of his son George the Great by the hands of those medical scum, who tortured and killed his beloved son George the Great. Every second the doctors remained breathing, living and breathing, Domenico's rage heightened to ferocious levels and extremes. Domenico Armando wanted them dead like yesterday, full stop!

Domenico Armando sat in perfect solitude for now the next evening inside his upstairs glamorous office of his most expensive home in New York City, worth $160 million located on Madison Avenue in the borough of Manhattan. The spectacular gothic mansion with its red glowing windows at night certainly matched Domenico's red hot fiery temperament at present. It was 10:00 PM at night, complete darkness outside. And as Domenico Armando sat inside his office in the dead of night, with his office lights shining on his enraged face, Domenico planned his great and terribly terrific retribution against every criminal medical practitioner and dirty bitch nurse situated in New York City, and the country, and **the world at large!**

Domenico Armando wanted to witness the corpses of every criminal doctor and every criminal bitch nurse lying down dead at his feet. He blamed those horrendous tragically corrupt scummy doctors and nurses for the death of his son, George the Great. And Domenico planned a great revenge against them and their disgusting practises, where they lay the foundations to make huge sums of money at the mental and physical expense of their victim patients. No patient was dearer to Domenico Armando's black heart than the dead former patient of such filthy maggot scum medical losers, which was his offspring, he called George the Great.

Domenico Armando poured himself a glass of Strega from the corner bar set up inside his office, and he lit himself a cigarette, as he sat on the leather sofa inside his great and magnificently high society furnished office, when he planned his attacks against every medical scum that lived and breathed across the entire globe, beginning with New York City.

Domenico Armando's manic eyes blazed as hot coals with fiery anger and devil-in-hell frightening rage at the thought of his son's victimisation by such despicable two-faced deplorable facades, such doctors and nurses portrayed within their professions, which cost millions and billions of patients; and no patient dearer to him-the Armando chief, than his son George.

Domenico Armando kept his son George's cremation ashes in his possession by his side constantly, inside a colourful glass vase, to witness the cremation ashes frequently inside - and reflect upon his emotions repeatedly fluctuating from sadness and anger and wanting revenge. His son George died at the early age of 21. And Domenico Armando wanted sweet retribution against everyone responsible for that horrendous crime of killing his son, especially every doctor and corrupt politician, such dirty politicians, who legislated policies which allowed doctors, criminal doctors, to practise their medical corruption throughout the country and the world itself quite visibly and terribly, as legalised criminals, getting away with their patients' slaughter by the masses and multitudes every day of their hypocritical and grossly mass murderous crimes they engaged inside their medical practises. It was a brutal calamity and a fucking catastrophe, Domenico Armando considered. The politicians were the scum of the earth who caused all this medical corruption. And the politicians were the scum of the earth who caused all the corruption in the justice system. It was the politicians who legislated evil legislative policies which allowed criminals to play with the justice system and get away with mass murder; the same way the politicians legislated criminal policies and criminal legislations which allowed evil doctors to in fact become what they truly were, legalised criminals and mass murderers of their patient victims!!!

The whole thing was a farce! It was a sham! It was scum doctors however endorsed to kill by the masses their patients by the very voted-into-office scum politicians! And Domenico Armando planned the death and destruction of every criminal doctor across the globe and every criminal politician across the globe, full stop!

Domenico Armando thought to himself: Yes, world. Yes, fucking scum world. You think my revenge so far was great and terrible against you all? But what you don't realise you scumbags in this world is that my revenge has only just begun! I have only just started my retribution against every criminal diabolical fucking lowlife, miserable piece of shit cunt that exists across this fucking world! My revenge has only just begun. My revenge will become more brutal, more explosive, claiming much more dirty lives which exists across this state, this country, and this entire fucking world! You all have seen nothing yet, you scums, you cretins, you motherfuckers, you cunts, you fuckheads, you shitheads. **I will fucking kill you hard,** Domenico Armando shouted out loud in his brain. His now sicker brain consumed with hatred and thoughts of retribution against those who wronged him through his family. For the death of my daughter Maria and for the death of my son George, this world is going to truly fucking pay. The scum in this world are going to exist no longer. I am going to tear out their fucking guts. I am going to rip out their body parts and spill their blood right at the spot where they stand. This entire city of New York is going to become a river, a blood pool of corpses of every scum I target, who deserves to die. And no dirtbag will get away any longer. No, Sir! No, no, no, no, no, no, no, no, no. No, you scumbags. You will not get away any longer. You hear me, you scum doctors in particular? It is your time to face death and destruction right now, you and the scum politicians who legalised your corruption to kill and destroy your patients - and steal their money before you kill and destroy them. You doctors are going to pay with your fucking lives! And so too will the politicians, who legalised your mass murdering crimes and scams and theft of your patients' money on a daily basis. You fucking scum doctors have been responsible for killing hundreds, for killing thousands, for killing millions, and for killing billions of your defenceless patients over the years. You scum doctors are cowards! You have no backbone! You are truly the lowest of the low! You are all filthy malicious contemptible two-faced hypocrites, who practise scumbaggery in your clinics! First, you plan to steal your patients' money - and then when you can steal no more, then...then you prescribe them lethal medications to finish your patients off, by slaughtering them slowly and painfully. And the patients cannot talk. The patients cannot walk. The patients cannot defend themselves. They cannot take you to court. And even if they can take you to court, the justice system is so corrupt, because of the scum politicians' horrible legislations, that guarantee the doctors will get away with their crimes anyway. As despicable judges will rule against the patients. And they will rule 'not guilty' verdicts of all the criminal doctors and acquit them of all their mass murderous charges and fucking conspiracies against the patients on the spot.

That is the injustice of the justice system, in which scum politicians have created in this country and in this entire fucking world. That is unacceptable. That is intolerable! That is something that will not be forgotten by me. That is something that will not be overlooked by me. Because the justice system of the world's courts is not a true and fair justice system. The justice system should not be called the justice system. Because the true definition of the justice system as it stands, is not a correct justice system. The justice system should in fact be called 'the injustice system!' Because that's what it is! The justice system is a terrible injustice against all victims. It is a joke!!! And the justice system only rewards criminals, delays court cases corruptly (at the criminals asking), and acquits them (the guilty ones), and allows them to get away with their horrible crimes of murder, mass murder, con artistry, theft, wearing two-faced masks. And the justice system with the politicians, helps to legalise criminal medical practitioners to torture and torment their patients, both mentally and physically. This is truly sickening. These doctors are not doctors. They are fucking zeroes. They are scumbags. They are fucking cunts. They are the lowest slime that anyone can find in this whole fucking world. They are worse than the rapists. They are worse than molesters. The doctors are the worst criminals and the worst scum that the world has ever seen!!! How? Why is that? Why have I deemed the medical practitioners to be the lowest of the low and the worst criminals the world has ever seen? Let me tell you fucking ignorant scumbags in this fucking world why I fucking came to that conclusion, that guilty verdict of all these medical fucking trash and scum, full stop! Because every other criminal is not infallible and can be destroyed.

But what makes the doctors worse is that their crimes are legalised by dirty politicians. The dirty politicians have legalised criminal medical practitioners and criminal nurses to steal and kill by hundreds, by the thousands, by the millions, and by the billions every single fucking generation of their despicable careers. The scum politicians were responsible for the corruption in the justice system, just as fucking sure as fucking hell, the politicians were responsible for legalising the crimes of every dirty medical practitioner across the whole fucking globe!!! But where do you think you're going to go you dirty doctors? And where do you think you're going to run to, you scumbag politicians with your evil legislations and your loopholes in the justice system, which allows doctors to escape justice for the death of their patients, just as you designed the justice system to acquit all the dirty practitioners of medicine to get away with the death of my wonderful handsome son George the Great. The doctors mistreated my son George the Great. The doctors misdiagnosed my son's condition. They abused my son, George the Great. The doctors intentionally misdiagnosed my son's condition and in turn, they intentionally prescribed him the incorrect medications. And they were laughing as my son's condition deteriorated quickly. Because his condition was a disease of the nervous system. And the nervous system is a horrible gruesome condition. When someone is struck with a neurological condition, the condition deteriorates at a much faster rate than terminal cancer. And the doctors intentionally caused my son to become so sick, that his handsome looks turned to gruesome ugliness. That in itself, such rapidly declining calamitous deterioration had truly crushed my son's spirits.

My son became a recluse after that! My son became embarrassed by how his condition made him look to the world. My son did not want to leave his house. My son did not want the scum of this world seeing him in such a diminished capacity, with his appearance transformed to unrecognisable monstrosity. But the doctors caused all this destruction to my son's mental and physical wellbeing. The doctors took my son's money, and the doctors intentionally misdiagnosed my son and intentionally prescribed incorrect medications to my son. And as my son's condition deteriorated rapidly…as my son's condition deteriorated at an alarming lightning speed rate, the doctors sat inside their offices and began laughing. They were laughing at my son's suffering. The doctors were laughing at my son's misery, suffering and the torture and torment such disgusting doctors had inflicted upon my wonderful victim son, who was their patient.

Where do you think you're going to end up, you filthy fucking doctors? Do you seriously think you're going to get away with what you did to my son? Do you seriously think you are going to live for much longer, to use my son's money to buy expensive food and fill your fat bellies at the expense of my son's corpse? No, you fucking dirty pig medical practitioner swine and scum nurses. No. No, you fucking creeps and human trash vermin. You will not get away with what you did! You doctors are going to suffer dearly for what you did to my helpless poor son. You doctors are going to pay with your fucking lives. Because it's not only my son that you killed, but you also hardened his father's heart. My heart! You have hardened me by your sick actions. And because you killed my son, you have triggered my emotions viciously and callously at that!!! I will kill not only you doctors and nurses, but I will slaughter your families! I will blow up your houses! I will blow up your cars! I will blow up your medical practises, your hospitals, your clinics and your entire fucking existences.

I will kill your siblings. I will kill your friends, your evil friends. I will slaughter your mothers and fathers and your grandparents. All your relatives who are still alive, will end up in the grave, as you put my son in the grave. And you have hardened my heart, because of all that you have done! So, you will all fucking pay dearly for that! You are all dead, you fucking lowlife piece of shit maggot scumbag fucking cunt, useless, worthless, no good for nothing, bags of shit medical practitioners and fucking grotesque ugly bitch nurses. You hear me??? You are all going to fucking pay for what you did to my son George. That's right. You are going to suffer! You are going to bark like dogs. I am going to torture you. I am going to spill your blood. I am going to amputate your arms. I am going to amputate your legs. I am going to tear out the fucking guts of all you hideous frauds. I am going to rip out your intestines. I will fucking tear out your livers, your kidneys, your fucking hearts, your black hearts; I will cut out with a knife. And send them to the police station. So, the police can then sift through that evidence of how the true justice system should be enforced. By my laws. And not idiot politicians' weak laws, of just simply throwing dirty pigs in prison or the electric chair. No, no, no, no, no. Prison bars or the electric chair is too quick, it's too swift. But what I have in mind, to torture you, and make you bark like the dogs before you die, that is true justice. I want to see you suffer. I want to see you screaming in pain, excruciating pain, for the death of my son George the Great!

You fucking scum doctors are going to know the true definition of pain. Because I am going to give you a dose of your own medicine. **The perfect prescription I have in mind for you scumbags!** You see, as you prescribe painful medications with lethal side effects that hurt and torture your patients, I will use my own brand of medicine to cure your corruption. First, I am going to torture you. I am going to make you scream in agony. I am going to torment you mentally. I am going to torture you physically. And when you are screaming in front of me, it will be a very long time of agonising pain and excruciating suffering before I let you scumbag fucking cunt doctors and fat bitch nurses finally enter your graves, dead as you all deserve to be!!!

So be ready, you world of scumbags. Because World War 3 is about to be unleashed by I-me-Domenico Armando, for the deaths of my beautiful daughter Maria and my handsome son, George the Great. My beautiful daughter Maria and my handsome son George the Great are both turning in their graves right now, crying and weeping to me. Wanting me, their father, to inflict justice against all the scumbags in this world who have wronged them - and who are responsible for their untimely deaths. My daughter Maria was a sweetheart, an angel of a girl who I loved dearly. And my son was also a prince at heart. Just like my daughter Maria, my son George, was never involved in my business. But he had other plans for his life. And I gave him my blessing, so he can proceed with his life legitimately and cleanly. My son had big plans for his future. And I was going to subsidise his plans as his father, who loved his children very much. But you robbed my children. You robbed my daughter. You robbed my son. You robbed my two beautiful children from their futures. My daughter Maria and my son George were killed by the scum in this world at very early ages. This world's evildoers killed my children when they were in the prime of their lives, in fact just beginning their lives. You robbed them of their futures. You robbed them of their destinies. You crucified my children. You destroyed my children. You tortured and tormented my children unjustly and callously. And that resulted in my children ending up in the grave at very early ages. And for that, I WANT REVENGE!!! For that, their father, I-me-Domenico Armando is going to exact his brutal onslaught against the scum in this world, until they bark like fucking dogs in excruciating agony, before I allow them to become corpses. And they will become corpses, mass corpses, that will be driven inside very, very overpopulated cemeteries. Yes.

Yes, indeed. But the slaughter of all you dirtbags will fill every cemetery in New York City, across the country, and across the entire globe. Every cemetery in this entire world will become at full capacity and overpopulated by your filthy corpses. That is how many lives I plan to destroy, as you have destroyed so many innocent lives in your horrible existences on this earth unjustly. But failed politicians and the failed justice system have criminally and evilly legislated you all to exist this way. Yes. Yes, indeed. Our dirty rotten filthy lowlife piece of scum motherfucking cunt politicians, are the ones truly behind all this corruption in all facets of our society, throughout this entire world! They legislated evil laws, just as sure as they legislated the evil policies of the disorganised and criminally immoral all-evil justice system!

Now, does the world understand why I despise politicians? Because it is the politicians who are responsible for all the callous crimes that exist in the world today, full stop!!! Let me reiterate over and over and fucking over again. Through horrible legislations and weak laws in the justice system, the politicians have basically created a justice system which is truly an injustice system. Which favours the criminals. And this disfavours the innocent godly creatures which exists in the world, such as my daughter Maria and my son George. Who used to exist. But now... yes, now, they are all now dead. All now pronounced dead in the grave by those despicable practitioners of evil. And those evil legislators of evil, who allowed it all to happen. Who are our dirty rotten scum lowlife fucking pig politicians existing in this country and in this entire fucking world!

No one will get away with anything this time! No one is going to escape death this time. And don't even think to stop me, Robert Stewart. Because my good friend Robert

Stewart, you are going to learn a very hard lesson, that my justice against the scum of this world, far exceeds any form of justice or any form of expectation in delivering justice, by your hands and your police station ever could even dream of finagling!!!

CHAPTER 7

Domenico Armando was extremely impatient. He wanted justice against his familial losses delivered on the double, on the spot, with no fucking delay! Domenico Armando took many drags of his cigarette and poured himself another glass of Strega. Domenico rose onto his feet and strolled to his local bar set up inside his prestigious office inside his Manhattan mansion in the dead of night. He poured himself two more shot glasses of Strega he skulled in an unsuccessful attempt to quench his emotions, now boiling with rage, at a world of scum and filth, he classified, who were responsible for the deaths and murders, of the good and the innocent, such as his daughter Maria and his son George the Great.

Domenico Armando wanted to witness the corpses of all the guilty responsible for the death and slaughter of his children, before he could blink his eyes three more fucking times! And Domenico Armando was adamant that the deaths of the guilty culprits and the guilty perpetrators was not good enough. He didn't want them to succumb to quick deaths. No, no, no, no, no, no, no, no! Because quick deaths in himself was too easy and too painless. But Domenico wanted to torture them first. He wanted to torture their minds. He wanted to torture their bodies. He wanted to witness them screaming in excruciating bitter agonies before he gave them the privilege, the final privilege, of death itself, inside their fucking coffins, which would shortly cause every cemetery across the entire world to be filled to capacity!

The manic-eyed Armando Boss was concocting a very wild and lunatic scheme to fill every cemetery with male and female dead corpses and their dead graves! The graves of all those he deemed guilty! Domenico Armando wanted them dead in the ground. Domenico Armando wanted all of them dead in the ground. Every filthy bag of shit, thieving publishing house rip-off merchant and con artist scamster, who stole from their author clients, as they stole the money from his deceased daughter Maria. And Domenico Armando wanted every dirty doctor and dirty criminal nurse across the entire fucking globe incinerated for the death, the brutal, cold-hearted death of his son, George the Great.

My beautiful daughter Maria and my handsome son George's tears will soon stop shedding. Because, by the very justice, the brutal justice your father has deliciously planned, in avenging your deaths, will certainly force you to stop turning in your graves in suffering. And I will gladden your hearts, my wonderful precious children. I will bring eternal justice for your horrible ends, your unjustified ends, my angel children of mine!

The world is going to suffer. The world is going to pay for what it had done to you. Yes, my wonderful children. World War 3 is on the brink of being declared by your powerful father, Domenico Armando! And World War 3 will be declared as surely as the existence of fucking hell, for what the world has committed, the sick and evil atrocities of murder of my children. Such sick crimes the world has committed against my wonderful and beautiful family tree.

You scum of the world tried to destroy the Domenico Armando legacy, by destroying the heirs to his throne. But no, no, no, no, no, you world of greedy thieving scums and murdering two-faced gutless cowardly trash heaps of shit; don't think for a second, you fucking trash heaps of scum existing in this world right now…don't think for a second, that you are going to get away with what you did to my children - and what you are continuously doing to innocent people in this world for one second longer. Because dirty politicians and their dirty inferior legislations and criminal legislative policies they have designed within the walls of the justice system, to help all you criminals be acquitted inside courts of law, will not be able to assist you from my justice. I will enforce justice, the sort of justice, this damn world should have always been participating in the enforcement of! My justified laws that should have always been enforced.

My justice will be to find all of you guilty. And to sentence you all accordingly, to painful screaming deaths. That is how justice should be enforced. My justice. Not the justice of dirty politicians, which isn't justice at all. It is only true injustice to all of humanity; all the innocent people of humanity have experienced the injustices of the justice system. But now, you're about to experience true justice, authored and founded by The Great Domenico Armando himself. My justice is the true justice system of the world. I am here in this world to enforce justice - and to become judge, jury and executioner! And fucking vigilante, for all the good people you guilty scum of the world have killed, as you have killed my daughter Maria and my son George the Great!!!

So, get ready to die, you filthy world of scums. Get ready to die, all of you publishing criminals who were responsible for the death of my daughter. There will be no more publishing criminals in this world. I am going to kill all of you practitioners of publishing theft and publishing con artistry, who con people to sign royalty stealing contracts. All of you practitioners of such stealing, thieving wickedness are going to become extinct! Your days are numbered. I am going to kill all of you. I am going to kill your families. I am going to kill all the bosses and all your staff members of all thieving publishing companies: all the criminals, liars, gossipers, slanderers and pieces of shit. I am going to blow up your publishing companies. I am going to kill and destroy every criminal publishing boss and publishing employee across the entire fucking world, beginning with the United States of America.

And then for the death of my son George the Great, every evil criminal stealing doctor, and evil criminal nurse, every stealing dirty ugly piece of shit pig nurse, is going to enter their fucking graves for the death of my son, George the Great. No one is going to get away. Be prepared you world of scumbags for World War 3.

And be prepared my staunchest worthy opponent Robert Stewart for the true war, the true battle of your life. Because you Robert Stewart are not going to stop me. You will never stop me! I am Domenico Armando. And Domenico Armando is bigger than life itself!!! I am greater than everybody combined. I am the greatest leader the world has ever seen. Remember that my worthy enemy opponent Robert Stewart. And also remember one more thing my archenemy Robert Stewart: all your brains and all your wartime skills will never be able to outfight, outsmart or outwit me! You will never outmatch me. You will never challenge me successfully again! Because I am going to defeat all your efforts to stop me, my dear good friend, Commander Robert Stewart! Because your brand of justice against the scum in this world, yes it might be effective, but it is still too lenient in its delivery against such fucking deplorables. Your justice is certainly too fucking lenient.

Because, what this world needs; what this world really needs; what this world truly deserves, is my brand of justice. The world needs my legislative policies to rewrite the justice system's weak and pathetic criminal insults to law and order. The innocent in this world needs me to enforce my unmercifully cruel, callously ruthless, and vindictively brutal forms of justice against every scum and every creep and every wicked practitioner that walks the streets unjustifiably in this world. The good and the wholesome…all the innocent across the entire fucking globe needs me to destroy all those terrible and horrible walking shitshows and human disaster zones, that has harmed them in unconscionable ways!

Because all these evil people my friend Robert Stewart, are just about to become extinct. So don't bother arresting anybody Robert Stewart. Don't bother bringing them before your fucking stupid justice system. Your corrupt justice system. Because let me tell you something Robert Stewart. I am going to get to them all first. I am going to slaughter them first. And all you have to do is thank me for making your job a whole hell of a lot easier, by eradicating those filthy maggots across this entire world, before you even have a chance to fucking arrest anybody else!!!

So, these are your orders from me Robert Stewart: Just sit back my friend Robert Stewart and enjoy the show. And don't try to stop me, my good friend Robert Stewart. Because I guarantee you my friend, your efforts will be unsuccessful. Like I said before my friend Robert Stewart, your justice is too lenient, full stop! Because the scum in this world deserves a whole hell of a lot worse, more severe penalties, than just prison bars and a slap on the fucking wrist by crooked courts of law and crooked judges, period! Yes, Sir. Nothing else. Nothing short of that. No, no, no. You see, what this world needs and what this world truly deserves, is my brand of unmerciful ruthless wicked, evilly ferocious, painful justice to be unleashed against every wicked scum and every fucking piece of shit creep that walks the face of this earth, and who walks this fucking earth unjustifiably.

Because these scumbags are going to walk the earth no longer. I will stop them. I will stop them dead in their tracks, my friend Robert Stewart. You hear me, Robert Stewart? You hear me, as you are stationed inside your police headquarters office, plotting hard and conspiring your cunning schemes to arrest all those scums.

Robert Stewart, just take a fucking vacation. Believe me. Believe your old friend Domenico Armando, when I tell you that you have earned a vacation. So, listen to me hard Robert Stewart. You will do as I tell you to do. You will follow my orders. I order you to obey me! So, get the fuck out of your police station office. Exit police headquarters completely and at once - and go and fucking take a vacation. Don't bother arresting anybody else. Just stop! Just fucking stop everything that you are doing right now, right this fucking minute, and leave police headquarters. Leave police headquarters immediately, right away. Right now, on the double. Right now. Right now. Right now. Right fucking now. These are your old enemy Domenico Armando's strict orders to you. And I insist, and I fucking demand, that you obey me and only me. Nobody else. You will do exactly as I tell you to do. You will follow my orders to the letter, effective immediately!

So, go. Take your wife and children on a very long vacation far, far away - and don't plan to come into New York City for a very long time. Take a vacation even out of the United States of America. And let me, your old enemy Domenico Armando takeover the justice system. Because the world needs me. The world needs Domenico Armando. I am going to take over the justice system, whether you like it or not Robert Stewart! Whether you decide to take your long overdue vacation or not. You can stay in your police office and continue to try to arrest these fucking felons. But Robert Stewart, you are going to find that your old enemy Domenico Armando will be doing the job that the justice system should have been doing from the very beginning: the quick painful systematic slaughter of all and every one of the targets situated inside your police station office, my good friend Robert Stewart.

But don't worry my old and dear friend Robert Stewart. Or would you like me to call you by your title, Commander Robert Stewart. If so, you don't need to worry about police business any longer Mr. Stewart. I will clear up all police cases. I hope you're going to be proud of my accomplishments Robert Stewart. Because I can guarantee you my friend Robert Stewart, that my form of justice is going to be a hell of a lot better than your form of justice, that you can deliver against those fucking pieces of shit motherfucking swine out there on the streets, living and breathing, and walking and talking, across this fucking earth and unjustifiably. Because these people are going to suffer. These people are going to pay. These people don't deserve to live any longer. Yes, my friend Robert Stewart. World War 3 is at hand. World War 3 is just a hair's breadth from being declared by I-me-Domenico Armando. I am the true justice system's clean-up crew. I will clean the world of every human filth that currently pollutes it.

Because your justice system Robert Stewart is too slow. Your justice system Robert Stewart is in fact a mockery of justice. Because you are abiding by sick and evil politicians' legislations. The police are forced to abide by sick and twisted policies, which are in fact, a true insult to the word, justice. You are simply enforcing justice of criminal politicians' laws. But if you were working for me Robert Stewart as my number one soldier, you will be given the best job of your career. I will personally equip you with the correct arsenal of bombs and of machine guns, to shoot first and forget about asking questions to these fucking scumbag criminals overpopulating the entire earth at present. And those garbage heaps, who are polluting the world's atmosphere wherever these pieces of human trash drag their fucking arses to, left and right, in every destination they walk, live and breathe, without deserving to walk, live and breathe anywhere whatsoever!

Because they will live and breathe and walk no longer. I am going to cripple their arms. I am going to cripple their legs. They will not be able to walk any longer to commit their crimes against good people, as they were allowed by your disgusting justice system Robert Stewart, to commit crimes against my daughter Maria and my son George the Great. And the rest of the innocent people of the world! Because every criminal will suddenly lose their arms and lose their legs. They will lose their ability to walk any longer. I am going to cut out their throats. And they will not be able to talk any longer, to conspire their evil conspiracies of theft and murder against innocent people. Just as they conspired and finally did murder innocent people, such as my daughter Maria and my son George.

You see, my friend Robert Stewart, all the evil is going to end in this world. It is going to end. By my methods. Because my methods are more efficient than your methods, the police force methods. So just take a fucking vacation Robert Stewart. Don't even think to try to stop me. Because even if I have to grab you Robert Stewart by your throat…and even if I have to force you to be knocked down unconscious onto the fucking ground, I will do it. Because make no mistake Robert Stewart about the seriousness of this situation right now. No one, no fucking person, not even the entire country's police force, and even the entire country's military soldiers all combined together, are going to get in my way from my great ambitions to deliver **True Justice** against every piece of scum that walks the face of this earth! And my justice will be unleashed against every creep and scumbag male and female piece of trash, which currently pollutes the world today.

So, stay out of my way Robert Stewart, or I will force you out of my way. I will kidnap you. I will hold you as my prisoner, until I get the job done. Don't force my hand, Robert Stewart. Don't force me to destroy you prematurely. Because I do enjoy our game together. But if you get in my way, you will force me to destroy you prematurely. And I would certainly regret destroying you too early. Because Robert Stewart... Because, I have a lot of plans for you! I still have to dish out my plans of bitter revenge against you for destroying my empire and destroying my family kingdom - and causing me so many losses in my plans to date. But I don't want you dead yet Robert Stewart. I want you still breathing. Don't you dare rob me of my entertaining revenge I have planned against you Robert Stewart. So, spare yourself a lot of trouble. Go and take a fucking vacation Robert Stewart and stay out of my way, or I will forcefully put you down. Because like I always said before Robert Stewart, my resources are a hell of a lot better and a hell of a lot more powerful than your fucking police resources. My resources can outmatch all of your law enforcement resources you can gather against me. I guarantee you that Robert Stewart. I cannot be defeated. I mean, Domenico Armando can never be defeated.

No one in this world can defeat Domenico Armando! Everyone else can be defeated and thrown into their graves, but not

I-me-Domenico Armando. I am one man Robert Stewart that you can never defeat, **KAPUT!**

And you will learn that the hard way Robert Stewart. You will learn that. I will stalk your world Robert Stewart, until I make you suffer as you made me suffer. I will unleash my revenge against you Robert Stewart and nothing will stop it. Your early death Robert Stewart will not come to pass. But your death by my hands will be a foregone conclusion! But not until…not until I have outlived my revenge against you for other wrongs you have done against me, Domenico Armando, KAPUT! AND KAPUT AGAIN AND AGAIN AND AGAIN!!!

But before I unleash my revenge against you Robert Stewart, I have a long list, I have a long list of deadbeats and filth bags on my death list that will be eliminated first. Those that have harmed me by harming my children, my dead children.

First, I will destroy them. I will destroy their homes, their businesses, their families, their friends, their loved ones and their pets. And then Robert Stewart I am going to come after you. I am going to test your skills to see how you will cope once Domenico Armando finally unleashes his final war against you Robert Stewart!!!

And it will be a delicious war! It will be a cold-and-calculated, very cruel war Robert Stewart, between Domenico Armando and Robert Stewart - and between Robert Stewart and Domenico Armando. And that my friend Robert Stewart is a beautiful war, a delicious war I am truly looking forward to! But first I am going to declare World War 3 against every publishing criminal employer and employee, and every medical practitioner criminal employer and employee - and no one is going to stop me!

I will wipe out the world of all the trash and all the conspired filth who put my daughter Maria and my son George into the grave. And who put them into the grave unjustifiably and maliciously and callously and ruthlessly. And by matching their evil deeds with my callous ruthless brutal evil actions that I will throw right back in their faces, this payment and evil payback, will become my perfect revenge, for their crimes and their sins they have committed against the Great Armando Family Empire! And to me myself personally: Domenico Armando!

CHAPTER 8

You have hardened my heart you world of scum, Domenico Armando thought to himself, as he remained in perfect solitude inside his Manhattan mansion office, planning his bloodbath-style retribution against a world in his mind, who wronged him. First, the publishing criminals who caused his daughter Maria's untimely premature death. The publishing criminals who ran the publishing industry criminally in an injustice-serving fashion against authors.

The publishing criminals attempted to steal the money from published authors instead of paying them the correct royalties. The publishing criminals also tried to steal the money from their publishing rivals. The publishing criminals also initiated con-job contracts to legalise their crimes of theft against published authors and legitimate publishing companies who were their rivals. And all the while, such publishing vermin were wearing masks, portraying themselves to the world as nice and decent people, but some of them were not even self-made. Some of them were frauds and scammers, who inherited large fortunes from their fathers. And used their fathers' money to invest in corruption and fraud by stealing the monetary profits that did not belong to them. They stole the money due to reasons of self-hatred they felt for themselves. They knew they were not worth even one cent to their names. They knew they were complete and utter failures and losers. They hated that authors were self-made accomplished people, so corrupt publishing proprietors (enlisting the assistance of their thieving staff members), tried to invest their money in lies and gossip against authors and their books, because they did not want authors to succeed with selling their books. Such publishing company criminal proprietors were grossly jealous that authors were successful, when they were not. They were jealous when authors were independently accomplished and they were not.

And some of these publishing criminal proprietors' self-hatred stemmed to great depths of miserable deficiencies they felt within themselves. Not only did they hate the fact that they were failures, but they knew they were nothing without their families' inheritances given to them. They were living off the back of their fathers' inheritances and using their fathers' money to invest in corruption and fraud. But such publishing company proprietors also hated themselves motivated by deeper feelings of self-animosity. A lot of them hated the reflection they saw every time they looked at themselves in the mirror. They hated their faces, they knew was just a picture of snake-rat ugliness. They hated their unmasculine slender bodies. They hated their weak breathless husky sounding pissant voices. They hated everything about themselves. And they took out their feelings of self-loathing and self-hatred inconspicuously against published authors in the field they were affiliated with, the publishing industry. They wanted to ensure that published authors did not succeed with their books and outshine them, because of their jealousies, motivated by their failures and the despising of themselves that ran rampant. This was how despicable and scummy so many people in the human race became. Playing con-job games and brain-dead schemes of lies and gossip against people maliciously behind their backs, because they did not want people such as great authors who wrote great books to succeed and outshine them. Just as such publishing crooks gossiped and caused slander against Domenico's daughter Maria, which eventually led to Maria's untimely and unfortunate death at an early age of just twenty.

But now all of you scumbags who tried to trash good and great people such as my deceased daughter Maria are going to have your entire lives crushed into the ground, dead, dead, fucking dead; in a pool of blood, I have prepared for all of you. Because I was the one who ripped the mask of your fucking faces! I exposed all your crimes! You scumbags don't have enough life experience. If you did, you would not have fucked with my daughter Maria! Domenico Armando thought coldly!

And also, the filthy doctors and the filthy nurses who play sick games with their patients, to steal their hard-earned money and misdiagnose them, and give them incorrect medications, so their already serious health conditions can continue to deteriorate rapidly, until the patients ultimately die!

Do you scumbag doctors and scumbag nurses participating in such mass killings of your patients, seriously think you are going to get away with your hideously vindictive, cruel and heartless murders of sick people, as you committed against my son, George the Great? No, you fucking scums. No, you fucking pieces of trash. I promise you...Domenico Armando promises you, that you will never get away with any vindictive crime and conspiracy and mass murders you have been responsible for committing, you dirty doctors and dirty nurses. Because Domenico Armando has prepared your graves! He has prearranged your funerals and predetermined your death sentences to come to pass very painfully and very excruciatingly. Which is exactly what you scums all deserve, for stealing the money from the sick and all your horrible medical fraud you unleashed against your patients, to ensure that they die prematurely; but not before you have first stolen their money for medical services which did nothing good for them. But only tortured them slowly. Tormented them painfully. And then ultimately killed them and caused them to become motionless corpses inside their graves.

But don't worry you scum doctors and trashy nurses. Domenico Armando has a beautiful and delicious plan of hellish retribution against all of you. Because your days of practising criminally in such a fashion, that callously caused the death of my son George, are swiftly coming to an end. Just as your lives are coming to an end swiftly and poetically by my hands and my hands alone! Your deaths are imminent. But before you all die, you are going to experience great pains and great agonies before I permit you the luxury of death itself. So don't try to escape... Don't go crying and screaming to the police for help. Because I assure you, it will be pointless. At this stage of the game, and since you have fuelled my unquenchable anger and wrath against you, I promise you one thing you dirty medical dogs, no one, no force on this earth will be able to help you - and would be able to spare you from your excruciating ends I have thus planned for all of you. Your fates and destinies are sealed. Your death sentences are preplanned by me. And your deaths are as certain, as is certain, that no police, no army, no combined authority on this earth, can prevent I-me-Domenico Armando from slaughtering each and every one of you motherfuckers and maggots, and sick cunts, fucking wankers, and useless, worthless pieces of shit, for the death of my son, George the Great! Just prepare yourselves for one outcome: pain. And with that will come destruction, loss and death of all your fucking lives!!!

CHAPTER 9

Domenico Armando not only planned to unleash World War 3 against his world of bitter enemies, but he also planned to counter what his staunchest enemy had in motion against him. Domenico Armando knew that Robert Stewart was also at the same time devising to unleash the next World War against him- Domenico Armando! It was just a question of who was going to strike first, and who was going to destroy the other by the first deadly and powerful piece of artillery and arsenal pointed and fired at the opponent adversary?

Domenico Armando insisted that he would defeat all his enemies including Robert Stewart, before his staunchest enemy in the game Robert Stewart could attack him first and foremost and bottom line, using his very powerful police arsenal pointed his way, and firing deadly bullets at his direction.

Domenico Armando was a master chess player just as his number one adversary Robert Stewart was a master gamesman in real-life chess. World War 3 was imminent between them. But Domenico Armando was on a fervent bloody campaign to unleash his wrath and retribution against all his world of enemies responsible for the death of his two beloved children in recent times, before his war against Robert Stewart would be declared violently between them.

Domenico Armando wanted to eliminate every dirty criminal thieving con artist piece of shit publishing criminal throughout the entire world, at the same time as he wanted to eliminate every criminal doctor and criminal nurse who killed their patients, the same as the publishing criminals and the medical vermin were responsible for the death of his children individually.

Robert Stewart was planning his elaborate strategic moves against Domenico Armando, gunning for him. Domenico Armando understood his number one opponent's methods and trademark all too well. Domenico Armando also planned to outgun Robert Stewart and his army of law enforcement men just the same, as Robert Stewart planned to machinegun the Armando Family Chieftain, with all his sick and twisted mass murdering butcher assassins he controlled in his criminal Armando Family Empire.

But Domenico Armando had a one-track vision in his mind. No one, not even Robert Stewart is going to stop me from destroying all those enemies who destroyed my daughter and my son in recent times. Every publishing criminal thief must be eliminated, just like every murdering doctor and evil nurse must be terminated - and at once!

Domenico Armando kept looking at his son George's cremation ashes sitting inside the glass vase before the porcelain coffee table situated before his leather sofa Domenico Armando was parked onto at this present moment in time in the dead of night. And Domenico Armando was consumed in his vendettas against all the doctors responsible for putting his son George into the grave. His mind continued its sick and vivid thoughts. I want complete destruction of my enemies. All of them! And I have found the perfect strategies to destroy them, before my enemy Robert Stewart can interfere in my plans once again - and foil my necessary revenge for the deaths of my beloved children. Now I see my son's cremation ashes before me and my mind unhelped is consumed with death and destruction I want to unleash against the world of medical scumbags responsible for killing him. All the doctors do is drug their patients to their eventual deaths! The doctors torture them the same way they tortured my son! I say fuck Medicare! It is money wasted to the scum doctors! Those doctors intentionally torture their patients, and they laugh about it all behind the backs of their suffering patients.

All you doctors and nurses deserve to die! To fucking die!!! And die you will at my hands! And so too will the scum politicians who legislated your corruption as legal. The doctors and the politicians are all legalised criminals and filthy terrorists! And the nurses are bitches, fucking witches! The doctors are sadistic cold-blooded sick arse fucking serial killers! I will slaughter you all! And Robert Stewart will not be able to do a thing about it!

Yes. My son's ashes in front of me will forever serve as a constant reminder of what the medical criminals did to him! And I will constantly speak to my son's cremation ashes as if my son can communicate with me, his father. Because I hear my son's words. I sense his pain at his early death by the hands of such medical criminals. And I constantly appease my son by speaking to him through his ashes, telling him that he will soon be resting in peace because his great father Domenico Armando has everything under control. His father, Domenico Armando is planning a great revenge against all those who wronged him and caused him to die prematurely, long before his time, at such an early age of 21, full stop!

Yes, my enemies in the publishing industry and my enemies in the medical community. Prepare to all be destroyed at my hands! **Because what I have planned for you is the true APOCALYPSE! Your complete destructions!**

And based on that fervent and cold-blooded declaration of wholesale revenge BLOODY MASSACRES against his world of bitter enemies at large, **Robert Stewart had currently declared the next World War against Domenico Armando!**